CAMP OLVIDO

CAMP

MIAMI UNIVERSITY PRESS

A NOVELLA BY LAWRENCE COATES

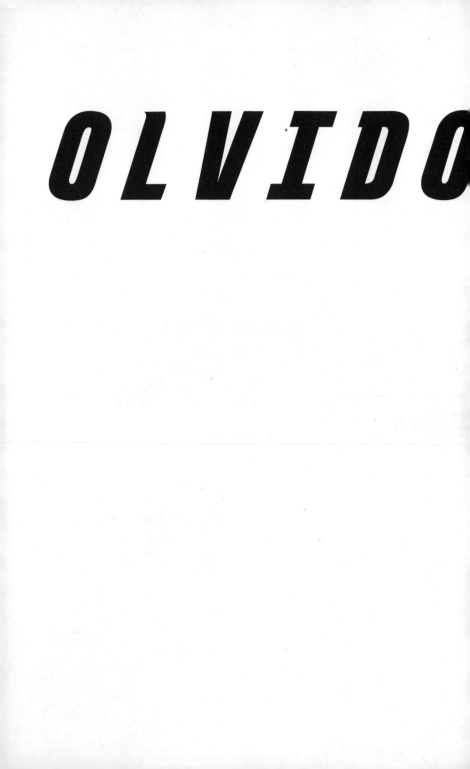

OLVIDO

COPYRIGHT © 2015 BY LAWRENCE COATES

EDITED BY JOSEPH BATES

EDITORIAL ASSISTANT: SAMANTHA EDMONDS

COATES, LAWRENCE, 1956–

CAMP OLVIDO / LAWRENCE COATES.

PAGES ; CM

ISBN 978-1-881163-57-2

(SOFTCOVER : ACID-FREE PAPER)

1. LABOR CAMPS—CALIFORNIA—FICTION.

2. LABOR DISPUTES—CALIFORNIA—HISTORY—

20TH CENTURY—FICTION. 3. MIGRANT

AGRICULTURAL LABORERS—CALIFORNIA—

HISTORY—20TH CENTURY—FICTION. I. TITLE.

PS3553.O153C36 2015

813'.54—DC23

2015023897

DESIGNED BY QUEMADURA

PRINTED ON ACID-FREE, RECYCLED PAPER

IN THE UNITED STATES OF AMERICA

MIAMI UNIVERSITY PRESS

356 BACHELOR HALL

MIAMI UNIVERSITY

OXFORD, OHIO 45056

FOR VICTOR VARELA

*E*veryone knew the sound of Esteban's car horn when it rounded into the camps in the evening, a two-toned horn, a low note followed by a high note, piping through the light dry breeze that cooled the darkening valley after another hundred-degree workday. He'd had the horn installed on his '28 Dodge so that the pickers would know he had arrived, know it was time to drink, to enjoy, to forget. At twilight, he drove down rutted lanes, along irrigation ditches, to where staggered lines of earth-hued tents and rude structures of cardboard and packing crates huddled together amid the vast fields of California cotton. He parked near weigh stations and sheds, set up a barrel of Jackass brandy that he sold for a nickel a glass, laid out bottles of wine for sale in unmarked green bottles, and the back bumper of his car became the center for a gathering of the sun-darkened men who had spent the week working through the fields with a cotton sack tied around their necks. They came and drank and built an open fire as the sky reddened in the west, reddened over a plain of drained lakebed and scraped tule marsh as flat and vast as the sea. Then the women came out, who had also been dragging ten-foot-long sacks through the fields, and children began to play on the edges of the flickering light. They marked as they could the end of another day in the cotton, a long harvest that might sustain them until the beginning of lettuce picking farther south.

Esteban leaned back against the bumper of his car as the poor celebrations gathered, grew, faded, not drinking himself but smiling and joking with the men who did. He wore a knife on his belt, a six-inch blade, the horn handle visible above the leather sheath, and even as he smiled his eyes were watchful, and he stuffed the money he collected into a leather pouch he wore around his neck. The following night, he would visit another camp, and the night after another, gathering in the stray coins left from the cotton tickets cashed in at stores in town.

At Camp Olvido, on a Thursday in early October, Esteban sounded his horn and parked beside the one permanent structure, a stable for oxen in times past. Rain had come through mid-week, and the tents were bowed more deeply, and the cardboard huts had that wavy brittle look of having been soaked then baked in the sun. They would not last through December. Esteban opened his trunk and set up his barrel, but nobody immediately came forward. He looked down the lines of tents and saw several black-haired children peek around the canvas at him then disappear. He reached in the open car window, blew the two-toned horn once more.

An old man emerged from the stable dressed in overalls and a blue workshirt, his white hair encircling his head like a tonsured friar's. He walked to the Dodge and planted himself before Esteban, his hands strong and clenched and his mouth drawn with the bitterness of years working under the sun.

Do you believe that God put us on the earth to suffer?

Esteban didn't know the man. He had seen him in Camp Olvido before but had never sold him brandy or wine.

No. I don't.

You sell lies. He pointed with his chin at the barrel standing up in the trunk. You sell the feeling that the world is kind, not alien to us.

I sell what the people want to buy.

Then you disappear with their coins, money that could buy bread for a child. Like *zopilote*, picking the bones from wolf kill.

Who is the wolf?

You know the wolf. You know the wolf very well.

Now a few men approached the car, though not with the normal smiles of greeting and anticipation. One man, tall and wearing a red bandana around his neck, took the old man by the arm and guided him away from Esteban.

Come with me. He looked at Esteban over his shoulder, asking him to be understanding toward an old man.

Esteban used a tin dipper to fill cups from the barrel and handed them to the men standing around him.

The first *copa* is on me.

Gracias. Gracias.

When all had a cup and had taken some quiet sips, Esteban pursed his lips toward the black doorway of the stable, where the old man had returned.

What is happening?

The men looked down, ashamed, reluctant to speak of their helplessness.

There is a child, one said.

What child?

A child stalked by death. A bright child. The only grandchild of the old one.

How many years?

Chiquito. The man held his hand down and crooked his finger upwards to show how tall the child was. Three years, no more.

And the old one blames me for this? What do I have to do with this sadness?

Esteban looked at each man, but none would meet his eyes.

What does this have to do with me?

Nothing. Nothing at all.

The man with the red handkerchief returned, and he held out a cup to be filled.

One nickel.

Of course.

The small group of men who drank remained quiet and somber, some leaving after one cup, others shuffling in. Two young men, Policarpo and Nivardo Del Río, brothers from Chihuahua, hovered close to Esteban. They were unmarried, and they had always been open in their admiration of Esteban, asking him questions about his car, about distilling brandy, about making wine, about living in town. Esteban noticed them staying near, even though they had run out of money, as though waiting for a moment to talk to Esteban alone, but he put them off. After an hour, the sun was down, and no small fire of celebration brightened the cleared space, and Esteban bunged the barrel with a cork stopper and wooden mallet, then slammed the car trunk shut.

Buenas noches, he said. *Buenas noches a todos.*

In the darkness, the stable glowed dimly. It was an old structure, long unpainted, and the boards between the posts had warped and shrunk and cast out their rusty nails, and from the gaps between them leaked the meager light of a kerosene lamp. Esteban walked to the grained and splinter-ing boards and leaned in to peer through an open crack. He saw a woman in one of the four stalls, sitting on a lumpy tick mattress on the dirt with a shawl about her shoulders. In her lap she cradled the sickened child like a bundle of sticks, arms and legs harrowed by hunger and dysentery. She held a soaked rag in her hand, and she was trying to drip water into the child's open mouth, but the child turned his head left and right and pedaled his legs, and from the kerosene lamp at the woman's knee, strange insect-like shadows played against the uneven walls. Behind the woman, the child's father stood with a hand on her shoulder. His face was thin and long-jawed, with a long horsey moustache covering his teeth, and his eyes were black and mad. About them gathered other women and, leaning over from the adjoining stall, the old man and the man with the red handker-chief around his neck. All watched as though watching with hope might itself be healing.

Esteban walked to the doorless entryway of the stable, stepped inside. The smell of burning kerosene, penetrating and noxious, could not mask the smell of the thin watery shits the child expelled, or of the shit-soaked rags the women took from the mother when she unwound them from the child's legs to rinse them in an irrigation ditch, replaced with other rags until they too were fouled. The ceiling of the stable was low, and even with the breeze let in by the gaps in the siding, the air was thick and fetid.

Esteban went to where the woman sat with the child and bowed his head to her, not from pity or awe but merely in recognition of a suffering he had seen before. The woman took no note of him, inclined only to her son. Esteban withdrew to the side of the man with the red handkerchief.

What is his name?

Manuel.

And the parents?

Isidro and Helena. I am her brother.

How many days?

Seven. And yet the child lives.

Esteban looked at the thinning boy, thinning as though already turning into spirit, and did not express his thoughts.

If we could get him to our home, there is a woman who could cure this, a great *curandera*.

Where is home?

Milagro Park.

Esteban knew of Milagro Park. It was a cluster of houses carved into a hillside near the mouth of a ravine outside of Los Angeles. The houses were brick with good tin roofs, linked by a winding dirt road and footpaths, and the street-car line reached the foot of the hill so that those lucky enough to be on at the brick factory could ride to work. Many of the houses had electricity, and the hillside sometimes glowed in the evening. For the workers chasing paydays from harvest to harvest, it was the promise of some stability, some sense of continuance, that led them to say when they saw the glowing hillside, *¡Qué milagro!* What a miracle.

He also knew the family could not leave Camp Olvido to go there. The *enganchista*, the labor contractor who had brought them to the camp, would not let anyone leave until the third picking was completed. He would find that they were in debt for their food and shelter, and only by remaining until the end of harvest and picking bollies, the half-opened bolls that were as much sharp-edged waste as they were fiber, could they earn a bonus and be free.

Esteban knew all this. In the dark, he took out his billfold and drew out a five-dollar bill, a calculated gift, an offering to buy the camp's good will on his next visit.

He stepped forward and kneeled in front of the woman so that he could look up to her, meet her eyes. She regarded him for a moment, distantly, then turned her gaze back to her child. Isidro, the child's father, watched him with eyes black and full, deep-set within his skull.

He laid the bill down before them.

A gift, he said.

For what? Isidro asked.

Medicine, perhaps. Perhaps a doctor.

Or a priest, Isidro said.

As Esteban left, he heard the old man's voice croaking after him.

What you want, you cannot buy. You cannot buy what you want.

- -

Saturday nights, Esteban did not make his rounds. Those with money made their way into the small railroad town of

Lux, named after Charles Lux, who with his partner Miller once owned vast tracts of land in the Central Valley on which to graze beef destined for the butchers of San Francisco. Their company and holdings broke up after their deaths, with only the small town along the Santa Fe tracks retaining his name. Hobart Whitley, the developer, had tried to change the name of the town to Jefferson, when he had imagined a landscape of small family farms across King's County, small landholdings loved and cultivated with almonds and peaches and grapevines. But his vision failed, and all the land became Glover land, controlled by Joshua Glover and a few large growers who also commanded the water rights of the Sierra rivers, and the name of the town reverted to what it had been when the railroad built the first depot.

Part of Whitley's vision survived in the town's layout west of the tracks. There was a tidy town square with a white gazebo shaded by oak trees, surrounded by small businesses—a jeweler, dress shops, a five and dime, a hotel, a drugstore. On a main street leading from the station, there was a grocery, a ballfield for children, the police station and courthouse, the King movie theater playing talkies. But the town of Lux had not survived as a center of trade for small landowners. It sustained itself on the nickels and quarters and dollars spent by the placeless workers who washed through the town with the harvests that fell at different times the length of the Central Valley. Town shopowners and merchants distributed leaflets in Spanish at the work camps, sometimes dropped leaflets over the camps from a crop duster, luring pickers in to spend some of their cotton money. But the merchants took the money with an ill will, resenting their dependence on the fieldworkers, whom they saw as wandering strangers. Restaurants would not serve them, and the movie theater allowed them only in the balcony, Mexican Heaven, and their children did not go to school or play in the park.

Esteban lived above a tractor barn that had been converted into a pool hall on the east side of the tracks, the part once known as Chinatown from the workers who had built the railroad, and now called East Lux. The pool hall was lit by bare lightbulbs hanging from the ceiling and reflecting harshly off the whitewashed walls, and in clear weather the big barn doors were opened wide to the street, a large box of white light beckoning men in from the dark streets to the four tables spaced out along the broad cement floor. The big room filled on Saturdays with cue balls clicking and voices calling shots and laughing and jibing at makes and misses. In the back was a bar that sold illegal wine, though it had been many years since the sheriff had raided the pool hall. The growers wanted it tolerated, just as they wanted Esteban's selling in the labor camps tolerated, to give the pickers some miserable joy.

Esteban leaned against a corner of the bar that Saturday and watched the games, the colorful balls endlessly racked and rolled and sunk and racked again. He watched the men who came to the bar and worried their money before buying a tumbler of wine, thinking how much they could spend that evening, how little they had, how they deserved something to drink and a few hours of fun. Esteban drank for free. He supplied the bar with barrels of brandy and wine from a winemaker hidden deep in the Isabella Valley, and the man who ran the bar, an elderly man named Castro, filled his glass whenever it was empty.

As he drank, the Del Río brothers walked into the pool hall. They were two of the younger men in the hall, both near twenty, not yet bearing scars on their hands, their backs not yet permanently stiff, their faces not yet leathered by the sun and the wind. They were dressed as everyone was dressed, in jeans and workshirts and straw hats with the *alas* rolled up on both sides. But they moved more fluidly than the older men, old at forty, who ratcheted around the pool tables. They paused until they spotted Esteban, then they nudged each other and smiled and came to the bar next to him.

Don Esteban.

Welcome, Policarpo, Nivardo.

They were the first two men he had seen that evening from Camp Olvido. He expected them to tell him whether the child Manuel had died, but they ducked their heads when he looked a question at them, grinned foolishly, asked for one glass of wine that they took turns drinking.

Is this wine that you bring yourself, Don Esteban? In your Dodge?

You know already that it is.

How nice it must be. To have a good car, to live by selling wine instead of picking cotton.

Esteban did not reply. He already knew where this talk would lead.

Don Esteban. It was the older brother, Policarpo, who spoke. Is there a chance that you might need some help?

Not at the moment.

With loading barrels, with making deliveries?

No.

Well. We have a problem. We thought you might help.

Yes? What is the problem?

You know the daughter of *el viejo* Gamio? The young one?

Yes?

She is *en malas condiciones*.

Well. Which one of you?

They looked at each other, looked down.

We don't know, Don Esteban. It could be either one of us.

Well, one of you will have to marry her.

But we don't know which one. And it is the fault of your wine.

Esteban called to the bartender, who walked slowly toward them, sliding a rag along the bar as he came.

Señor Castro, are you responsible for the foolishness men do after drinking the wine you sell them?

Castro began to laugh, and his eyebrows, jet black under his cap of steel grey hair, shot up. If so, I have more sins on my back than you can count.

If you take us on as helpers, we could make some money. More than picking cotton. To pay for the child no matter whose it is.

I make less than you think. Am I living in the large house at the end of a lane shaded by cypress?

No.

I don't make enough to pay one helper, let alone two.

Esteban picked up his glass of wine and drank it down.

Señor Castro. Please give these two a good drink, at my expense.

He walked away, hearing their subdued thanks at his back. He passed the pool tables and the shooters, all engaged in their games, and walked into the street.

La Posada, two blocks south, bled a dark and reddish light through the painted windows of an old storefront, exhaled the smells of sweat and cigarette smoke and perfume. Inside, a single overhead fan turned slowly above the dozen tables, where groups of two or three men sat with women who laughed with too-wide mouths. The men complained about the field bosses, talked about their homes far away, flirted with winks and jokes. The women played coy, or reached out to stroke the shirt collar of the man closest to them. They always had a drink, and when they'd finished one, they signaled the bartender who brought another. When one thought a man was ready, she nodded her head toward the stairway leading upstairs and said, *¿Nos vamos?*

Esteban walked through the tables to the bar, and several women turned their heads. He was known as a *contraban-dista*, a bootlegger, someone who had found a way out of fieldwork, someone with cleaner hands and more money than the others. He rested an elbow on the bar and the bartender, a tall and gaunt man with sunken cheeks and skin strangely sallow from the lack of sun, asked him what he wanted.

One beer.

Coming up.

Esteban rested his back against the bar, looked over the room. A guitar that he had never seen played was hanging from one wall, and other walls were hung with thin plates of metal enameled with advertisements for tobacco and soft drinks and automobiles, the bright lettering dulled by grime and smoke. From the crudely adzed beams holding up the roof, spirals of yellowed flypaper dangled and waved slowly in the sluggish air.

A bottle of beer clicked on the bar behind him, and he turned and pushed a dime and a nickel across the dark wood. The beer was icebox cold, and it foamed when he drank, and he wiped his mouth with the back of his hand after he put it down.

Then there was a woman beside him, a fleshy woman who wore a black skirt tight around her full hips and an orange-and-black blouse low and frilled in the front, and she leaned over the bar next to Esteban so that her breasts were round and obvious.

Hola, Esteban.

The bartender immediately placed another bottle of beer in front of her and turned his pale face to Esteban.

Twenty-five cents.

Ladies' drinks always cost extra. Esteban flipped a quarter onto the bar to go with the fifteen cents he had just put down, and the bartender clawed it all into his left palm.

Thanks for the beer, *cariño*. Do you have a cigarette?

Esteban slipped the little bag of Drum tobacco from his pocket and she nodded approval. He rolled two cigarettes, held one up to her face, and she took it between her purpled lips. He lit hers and his own, then turned to look over the room.

Ah, María. When are you going to let me take you away from this vale of tears?

She laughed. You wouldn't know how to live anywhere else.

What do you mean? I could live like ordinary folk.

No. You need to live in the Valley, bringing wine and brandy, bringing a little party with you wherever you go.

Not forever.

No?

Someday, I want to live back in the village.

What village?

It doesn't matter. Some village with a plaza and a market and a house with clean white walls. I could go to work in the cornfields every day, and you could stay home. Washing, ironing, watering your garden. And I'd come home to plenty of hot tortillas, *chile molido*, some chicken in the pan.

María laughed again and drank some of her beer.

You are so bad.

Me? Why?

For talking such fantasies that you don't believe. You, working in the cornfields?

With the love of a good woman, I could do it.

Let me tell you. If you went back to the village, you would soon be bringing in liquor on the sly, and selling it, and then looking for a bar like La Posada.

Would I do that?

And leave your little wife crying at home.

Oh, your bad opinion of me wounds me.

To live in a village like that, you have to care about someone other than yourself.

María, you know me so well. You are the woman for me.

Ha. For one night, *quizá*.

As Esteban turned to pick up his bottle of beer, the doors of La Posada swung wide open, and Diamond Peterson appeared in the dim red light.

Tssst. María hissed a warning to Esteban.

Diamond paused on the threshold, a tall man with muscle strung along his frame. Then he moved into the room like a large and graceful cat, muscled and fluid, and his white face and cropped blonde hair broke through the dense red air like a flame. At the tables, the dark fieldworkers bent down and pretended not to notice he was in the same room as them.

Esteban hunched over his beer, but Diamond came right to him and cast an arm over his shoulders, then looked past him to María, weighed her with his eyes.

Esteban! How is business?

Business is good.

Is it? Good. Then you can buy me a drink.

The bartender drifted over, his eyelids down in his sunless face, and placed a beer on the bar. Diamond ignored it.

What's your friend's name?

María.

María. Diamond switched to speaking Spanish. What do you think of Esteban? Is he generous?

Yes. María spoke in a small voice. He is.

And he should be. He makes money hand over fist. And if Mr. Glover tells him to sell more, he is glad to do so. And if Mr. Glover tells him to sell less, tells him too many pickers are too drunk to fill their bags, he is glad to do so. Not like that other *contrabandista*. You remember him, Esteban?

Who?

The bootlegger who came to the camps before you. Asunción Flores. Did you ever know him, María?

Asunción Flores? No, I don't think so.

No? Diamond made his face look surprised. Asunción never came into La Posada, talking big, acting like King Shit? He never came and sweet-talked you?

No.

That's too bad. He used to be a handsome man, like a movie star. Long straight nose, smooth skin, black eyes. Do you remember him now, Esteban?

Yes. I remember him.

I wonder where he is now. Diamond picked up his beer and drank with a thoughtful, musing look. I wonder. With his crooked nose and broken hand. Maybe laying railroad track in Arizona. But you won't end up on *el traque*, will you, Esteban?

I don't plan to.

No. You're too smart for that to happen to you.

He put down his half-finished beer and clapped Esteban on the shoulder.

Have a good time tonight, Esteban. I'll see you later.

On his way out, he stepped behind Esteban and patted María on the back and ran a hand down her bare arm. She shrank into Esteban. Diamond grinned.

You like them a little *gordita*, don't you?

Then he was gone, catlike, through the door. At the tables in the dark red light of the bar, the faces of the men slowly turned up, turned like pale lamps facing toward Esteban, a dozen faces shined with sweat reflected the bar's murky light back at him, dark shiny eyes fixed on him.

Esteban turned, and the bartender stood before him, waiting. When he spoke, only his mouth moved.

Fifteen cents. For the beer of the *señor*.

Esteban scowled and dug for two coins and rattled them onto the bar.

Hasta luego. Hasta luego, María.

Wait. Stay awhile. Have another drink, you'll be all right.

I'm all right now, he said.

- -

Esteban walked out onto the dirt-and-gravel street in front of La Posada, walked quick and aimless past other dim bars, past other bright and blinding pool halls. Above the streets, a crisscross of power lines swayed from poles, and occasionally a street lamp cast a pool of milky light. Beneath one lamp, a street vendor had set up an oil drum with a hole cut in the side and a woodfire burning inside of it, and he was using the metal top to fry onions and peppers and beef and keep warm a few small tortillas. Esteban stopped at the vendor and nodded, and the man expertly scraped some fried food into a tortilla and pinched it shut to make a *taquito*. Esteban ate it in three bites and asked for another. The vendor shoved some already-cooked food from the piles at the perimeter of the drum to the center. The food sizzled as it hit the hot metal, and he spread it flat, then pushed it into another tortilla.

How is business?

Sometimes good, sometimes bad.

But better than picking cotton.

I have picked cotton. Grapes, apricots, prunes, lettuce, apples, oranges, walnuts. I have picked this entire state, and California has used me up. I'm no good for anything but this.

Why don't you go home?

To where? To Mexico? Back to the bleeding heart of the world? No, there is no such home for me. Look.

From within his shirt he brought out a piece of wood strung from a leather cord around his neck. The wood was dark and smooth from having been handled many times.

This wood is from the cross in the church where we took refuge in 1912, when the wars reached my village.

What happened to the church?

It burned down. The priest refused to leave and died inside.

Was he a good priest?

No. He stole from the people.

Maybe that's why he didn't come out. Because he knew what would happen to him.

Many of us left the village after that. For the city, or the north. Scattered! I don't know where any of them are now.

Another man emerged from the darkness of the street, his features flat and washed-out beneath the lamplight, but Esteban recognized the red handkerchief around his neck. Helena's brother.

I have been looking for you, he said.

And you have found me. *¿Y qué?*

Helena's brother frowned. The child is still with us. I thought you might like to help.

I did help. I gave your sister five dollars.

Will you come with me?

Esteban looked at the street vendor, who handed him another small warm taco. He bit off half and chewed.

Where? he asked when he had swallowed.

Just a little ways. To see what happened with your five dollars.

Esteban put the other half of the *taquito* into his mouth and paid the vendor. He tapped his hip to feel the knife he carried there. Then he shrugged.

Let's go.

They walked back through the narrow streets, through darkness from one puddle of light to another. They passed small snarls of men coming out of the red-light houses, out of the pool halls. The men argued about where to go, and their arguments had a whine of frustration in them.

Helena's brother led Esteban down an alleyway between warehouses that fronted the railroad tracks. Esteban could see, through the small narrow frame of walls, a glow from the city of Lux, from the marquee of the movie theater, from the Owl drugstore, from the lights around the city park, from the houses. And he wondered if Helena and Isidro had somehow found a doctor who would treat Manuel for only five dollars, there on the other side.

They came to the tracks, leading north by east, south by west, with a dull metallic shine across the creosote-soaked crossties, drawing together before vanishing in the dark surrounding the town. Helena's brother led Esteban up a wooden staircase to one of the covered loading docks running along the tracks. The large square doors that led from the warehouse were all closed, like a row of empty faces, and against the wall between the doors, they came to Isidro. He was sitting on the dock with his legs angled out, a gallon bottle of wine by his side, gazing across the tracks. When he heard them, he pushed himself upright and faced them both.

So this is how you spent my money? Esteban asked. On wine? On getting drunk?

No, Señor. I tried with your money.

It's true, Helena's brother said. He tried to give it to the *mayordomo*, to let him leave, just leave and take his family home.

He laughed at me, Isidro interrupted. He said if he let everyone with a sick child leave, the cotton would never be picked.

He stooped down for the bottle of wine and took a furious drink. Then he smiled without humor and offered the bottle. Esteban took it, drank cautiously, and handed it to Helena's brother.

How can I help? Does he want a bigger *mordida*? I am not a rich man.

No, Señor, Helena's brother said. We need to talk to the boss of the *mayordomo*.

The boss of the *mayordomo*?

You are the only one we know who knows these people. You are allowed by them, and you yourself pay them a *mordida*. Don't deny it.

I don't deny it. But it will do no good to talk to him. There is a boss on top of that boss, and another boss on top of that. There is the grower, Mr. Glover, on top of that boss, and on top of Mr. Glover, a bank in Los Angeles. And you know what the bank says?

What?

Pick the cotton.

Take me to see the biggest boss you can, Isidro said. I will talk. I am the father of a son who is dying.

You think they care?

God cares.

Esteban took the bottle, drank. Exposed and belittled by Diamond, and bitter at being exposed, he decided he would gladly see someone else's life embittered.

I will take you to see Mr. Walker. But this favor I do for you is no favor. It will only show you how little they think of you.

He handed the bottle down. Isidro cradled it between his hands and looked across the tracks toward Lux, tense and baleful.

- -

Joe Walker drove a pickup truck over the gravel road that cut between the fields of cotton, headed toward one last weigh station. Walker was thick-bodied with a face permanently chapped and reddened by the sun and wind, hair crew cut into a thick blonde stubble. He kept a chaw of tobacco in his left cheek and from time to time spat out the open window as he drove. He was from Georgia, had followed the cotton west when he'd heard that the yield was three times higher in California, and after ten years in the Tulare Basin he was a supervisor, boss of five thousand acres, responsible for the profit and loss from that section.

He drove, uneasy about the man sprawled in the passenger side of the pickup. Aaron Glover, son of the big boss, sent to learn the cotton business on the ground in the drained lakebed that had made his family wealthy. Aaron was tugging at the yoke of his collar, shifting in his stiff new bib overalls. Walker was Aaron's boss, but neither of them forgot who Aaron's father was.

The sun in the west was low and bloated and red, and the land was so flat that no hills broke the horizon line. The truck had a metal visor built over its windshield, but they both squinted when Walker muscled the truck right onto a rutted dirt road.

Where are we going? Aaron asked.

Check the weigh station.

Oh. Another weigh station.

Tell you what. Walker tilted his head to the left and shot a stream out the window. Them weigh stations is what it all comes down to. Until you get the cotton in and weighed, all you got is possibilities. You could get rain or storm that'll knock things down. I've even seen hail. In September.

In Georgia.

Don't matter. It can happen. And pickers will try and pull shit on you too.

Like what?

Like throw things in their sacks, make 'em weigh more. Clods of dirt wrapped in cotton. Rocks. Wild melons. Wine bottles.

Wine bottles?

Some of them bindlestiffs we got wouldn't pick without wine. They'll take a drink, cork the bottle, and heave it a dozen plants up, then pick like hell to get to their next drink.

So do you check every sack?

Naw. We just set the scale back about five pounds.

He grinned at Aaron, and his teeth were brownstained and crooked.

We know they do it, and they know we do it. It evens out.

Tough luck for honest pickers, I guess.

Honest pickers? Hard to find.

Walker slowed the truck into the camp and cut a circle so that the truck was facing out the way they came in. He and Aaron got out and slammed the doors shut, then walked toward where the foreman stood beside a big spring scale set up on a tripod.

Who's the foreman? Aaron asked.

Name's Moose. He's good. But we weigh the cotton again at the gin, check the weight against the number of tickets he handed out.

Make sure it evens out.

You got it.

A long line of pickers waited to have their cotton sacks weighed. The young, eight or ten years old, had six-foot cotton sacks draped over their shoulders like giant sausages, thicker than a tree trunk, filled with enough white fluff to match their own weight, a hundred pounds. The men and women had longer sacks, patched and painted, dragged along the ground behind them. The strongest pickers managed four hundred pounds, collected pinch by pinch under the sun.

Walker and Aaron joined Moose at the head of the line as the workers emptied their sacks into the scale. The faces of the pickers looked up as the needle on the dial swung and settled. White faces, thin and whiskered, old-seeming because of missing teeth and pinched-in mouths. A couple of black faces, men who had found their way west and knew the seasons of cotton, men who might find the small wages of picking in California better than the endless debt of sharecropping. Mostly faces from Mexico, young and old, families with grandparents and young children, all trudging forward with their day's work a burden on their backs or on the ground behind them.

After seeing the cotton weighed, Walker and Aaron returned to the truck and bumped along the roads back to the high-sided building where the cotton gins were. In a corner of the building, a small office had been roughed in with two-by-fours but never completed, so that it jutted out onto the poured concrete like an odd skeleton, the single desk and two chairs and filing cabinets always on display. Walker ended days in the office, entering numbers in a ledger book and complaining that he farmed more with a pencil than a plow, and since Aaron had come on, they spent time there after being out in the field and talked over acres picked, pounds, bales, yield, the harvest. That evening, they sat in the office chairs with the large green ledgerbook spread between them and entered figures from the camps they had seen during the day.

Outside the high-sided building, Esteban was hesitating at the doorway, Isidro just behind him. He thought he had made a mistake in bringing Isidro here. He knew what Mr. Walker would say, knew that this was a futile errand. He had only wanted to show Isidro his place in the order of things, as Diamond had done to him. Yet Isidro seemed convinced that something miraculous would happen, and that worried Esteban.

Is he here? Isidro asked.

Yes. That's his pickup.

Then let's go.

Esteban opened the door. They both entered softly, al-most tiptoeing beneath the high dark walls, the towering shapes of machinery, like children entering the house of a giant. The office was the only space lighted in the building at night, and it threw crazy barred shadows onto the walls and ceiling. They walked toward the office, saw the two men, one standing, one lounging, waiting for them, and they both took off their hats as they walked into the cage-like space.

Buenas noches, Mr. Walker. Esteban nodded his head to Walker. He did not recognize Aaron, who had not gotten up from his chair, but he nodded at him as well.

It's you, Walker said, not unfriendly. What is it?

Who is he? Aaron asked.

Esteban Alas. He's a bootlegger who goes 'round to the camps on most all of your father's property.

A bootlegger! Aaron sat up, enormously amused. So you take wine around to all our camps?

Yes, Señor. Wine and brandy.

And brandy! Well, I hear that without your efforts, our cotton would not be picked. If they didn't know that a drink was waiting for them, the pickers would never wait in line with a cotton sack to be paid. We owe you a debt of gratitude.

This is Mr. Aaron Glover, Walker said. He looked at Esteban significantly, raised his blondish eyebrows as he punched the last name.

Isidro could not speak English, but he understood the name. Is that the son of the landowner? he asked Esteban.

It must be.

This is a sign.

Wait. Esteban had not expected to see Joshua Glover's son sitting at a desk with Joe Walker, and the meeting had now become risky, perilous. We cannot ask him. He is too important.

Is he more important than my son? No, this is a sign. He is a son, and he can save my son. Ask him.

It will do no good.

Ask him. I'll talk, you tell him in English.

Isidro's fevered eyes made clear that he would not leave without an answer. Esteban turned and bowed his head to Aaron. It is an honor to meet you, Don Glover. An honor.

It's too bad you didn't bring a bottle with you. We could have all drunk to your health.

Walker frowned at Aaron's odd mixture of condescension and familiarity. So what do you two want? he asked. Who's he?

Don Glover. Esteban spoke directly to Aaron. I present to you Isidro Rulfo. He has a request he would like to address to you.

To me? I feel like royalty. Well. We shall hear your request.

As Isidro spoke, Esteban translated into English.

I came to this country with my young wife, and the pain of my life had been not giving my wife any children. She had not been happy without a child to care for. Twice, she lost children before they were born. Finally she had a boy that we named Manuel.

Walker's eyes grew dark and sharp as he heard the Spanish, then Esteban's simple English. What kind of shit is this? he asked. What are you bringing this here to us for?

Aaron held up his hand. Let them finish. We've heard them out this far.

Isidro looked at Esteban, who nodded his head.

Ten days ago, in Camp Olvido, Manuel grew sick with a sickness we see every year in the camps. The children turn from bright flames, dancing and reaching higher, to dull earth. When they die, they look shriveled and dark, like the earth, and their spirits are gone. But Manuel's spirit remains. He is a charmed child, perhaps, and he lives. We want to take him home to a *curandera*, who might make him well. But the contractor and the *mayordomo* will not let us go. We ask you, Don Glover, to allow us to go, to tell the *mayordomo* to let us stop our contract and go.

So that's it, Walker said. Esteban, I thought you were smarter than this. Who do you think you are? You think you're someone who can come in asking for favors?

No, Señor.

'Cause you're not. You're just a penny-ante bootlegger. You think we owe you something?

No. I don't.

Then why do you come waltzing in here with this sob story? What made you think we wanted to hear it?

Wait a minute. Aaron, still sitting, raised his hand again. Let me see if I understand this. Their kid is sick, so they want to skip out on their contract and see a '*curandera?*' What's a '*curandera?*'

Hell if I know. Some kind of witch doctor. They believe in all kinds of shit.

Aaron began to chuckle. A witch doctor? Oh, that's rich. That's too much. I can't wait to write my friends about this.

37

Isidro watched Aaron laugh, not understanding what had been said. Has he said yes or no? he asked Esteban.

Not yet. But he does not show sympathy.

Ask him.

It will do no good.

Ask him, yes or no. In the name of God.

Esteban looked at Isidro being laughed at, and he saw a madness in his face. The meeting was turning out worse than he had imagined. Now all the managers of Glover's land, all the white people, would think him undependable, would think of him as the one who had breached the unspoken boundary of what was allowed him. Still, with Isidro's black and bloody eyes on him, he turned to Aaron.

Don Glover. He would like to know, yes or no.

Yes or no?

In the name of God, he asks it.

Walker spoke up. If we let everyone with a sick kid light out, we'd never get the cotton picked.

All right, all right. Aaron leaned back in his chair. Walker was admitting that it was his decision to make, that he was the owner's son and could do as he liked. But anything he did would be reported back to his father, whether he caved to a sob story or whether he knew how to be a hard ass. And he knew how his father would want him to act.

He leaned forward and shook his head at Isidro. Mr. Walker is correct. We have to get the cotton picked. And it sounds to me like your child is getting better. He's probably past the worst of it.

What does he say?

Esteban shook his head, said nothing.

What? Tell me what he says.

He says that Manuel is getting well.

But he is not. He still lives, but only by grace.

They don't care. It's as I said. No matter what you ask, they will say the cotton must be picked.

Isidro looked at Aaron Glover, sitting behind the desk in the wooden chair. Aaron leaned back, and the chair squeaked as it reclined, and he spread his hands as though he were helpless, as though he had done all he could possibly do.

Isidro asked Esteban, Will I see a bigger boss than this?

No. Never in your life will you see a bigger boss than this.

Isidro nodded and took one step backwards.

Esteban felt the knife being slipped out of the sheath at his belt. He felt it before he understood it, felt the slight tug on his belt and then the smooth slide of the blade against leather until it was freed.

With the knife in his hand, the father of the agonizing child did not pause for speech of threat or persuasion. He saw through the mild white face of the man costumed in bib overalls, sitting with an air of careless security after having adjudicated between life and death. He saw through to the deceiver, the adversary, and in his despair he lunged with the knife.

Aaron lifted his hand against the heavy scything blade, and it reaped off his small finger. He screamed at the sudden pain, the blood that was his blood, the transfigured man before him. The man scrambled over the desk, seeking more blood and quickly, and Aaron crouched and cradled his new-crippled hand dripping red to his chest, backing up. The knife blade swiped right and left before his face, keen to leave him forever marked. He shoved himself between the two-by-four studs and squeezed outside the caging office, onto the gin floor. One arm thrust out after him, long and weird and flashing steel.

Then Walker, a tower of flesh over the knife bearer, tackled Isidro from the side and bore him down onto the cement floor, and pinned the small and furious man beneath him. The knife fell free and skittered along the floor near the desk. Walker rose like a mountain and drove a fist down into the gaping face below him. He did it again, driving down as if to crumple the head against the floor.

Outside the office, Aaron held aloft his maimed hand, aghast.

Who is he? he shrieked. Who are these people?

Here he is, Walker answered. He hoisted the body of Isidro up from the floor and shoved his head between the studs toward Aaron, like a head in the ancient stocks, ready to be degraded. His face looked broad and clownish, already hammered into flatness, with the jaw slackened and the teeth lined with blood.

What kind of people are these?

Here. Right here.

Aaron gripped the stub of his little finger, slowing the blood from it, and neared his face to the face of the one who had robbed him, as he saw it, studied the way the blows from Walker's meaty fists seemed to have smeared the face into a mask of itself, at one remove from human.

Isidro's jaw began to work, but like a puppet's jaw, jerky and mechanical. It closed, then puffed out a bloody gob of spit.

Aaron wrenched back, then plowed an appalled fist into the battered face.

There you go, Walker said. There you go.

Esteban, still in the office, watched Aaron Glover raise his hand and bring it down upon the now helpless man, heard Glover emit a high and wild cry. Walker turned his head to look at Esteban, as though suddenly recalling another player was present, looked at him and at the knife still on the floor.

That your knife?

No, Esteban said. I didn't know he had it.

Walker gave a short, disbelieving laugh. Well. Either way, you're fucked.

Aaron staggered away from the unfeeling face to a dim corner of the gin building, and doubled over, and began to vomit a thin and bitter gruel.

- -

The courthouse was the tallest building in Lux, brick above sandstone with cryptic Masonic symbols and the date of construction engraved in the cornerstone. It was set back from Main Street behind a broad parterre, three stories high with a Victorian belfry rising incongruously from the gingerbread roofline. The main doorways were approached by ascending a monumental staircase and passing beneath a frieze of blind Justice, holding a balance scale in her right hand and, in her left, a sword.

In the basement of the courthouse, in the dark below street level, barred cages for men lined the outer walls, holding pens for drunks who would sober up in their own puke and urine until they could be hustled upstairs to stand sick-eyed before Judge Harkin. A deputy would hold the men upright while the judge asked what spread they had been working on. Guilt was never a question, and the sentence was always the same—thirty days picking cotton and a fine, or thirty days in the hole. Men always took the cotton, and the judge, popular with landowners, always won re-election.

Esteban and Isidro were pushed into the same cell, a six-by-nine space, iron bars from the ceiling to the concrete floor, with a narrow bench and a bucket for slops all the furnishings. Isidro got no doctoring on the way to jail. He sat on the hard plank bench, his clothes scarped into rags, his face masked in blood, skin peeled and revealing the abject flesh and veins beneath.

Esteban paced by the bars, waited for the chance to speak with someone, to try and talk his way out. There was little light in the basement jail. Three glowing bulbs hung from wires above the walkway that ran between the cells, and a barred half-window at the end of the walkway let in a sickened light from above ground. Esteban ran his hands along the cold bars as he walked back and forth, brought his palm to his face and smelled the sharp dry oxidization of iron. From time to time he looked at Isidro, who sat silent and fallen.

When the barred half-window was black with full night, drunks began to be herded in, groups of three or four stinking in their own filth, upright only because they leaned against each other and a deputy. At first, each round of collars was slammed into a separate cell to sleep it off, groups of ricket-thin white men with wispy beards and distant eyes, or Mexican men who had lost their hats and were covered with the dirt of where they had fallen. Then, as the night deepened, new detainees were pushed in anywhere, and fights broke out over floor space, and if a drunk in his sleep loosed a delusional scream, he was quickly silenced by a boot to the face or a thumb to the neck. Impromptu alliances formed, to guard against being preyed on, and each cell split into hostile factions, struggling through the night over the few square feet where their actions had borne them.

Esteban watched each group come in, tried to ask them what they knew of the mutilation of Aaron Glover, but they had heard nothing, and the deputies only smirked at him.

He waited for his cell door to be opened, for the dirty and feeble and incapacitated to be shoved in upon him and Isidro, but it never happened. Even as the surrounding cells filled with men, their cell was set apart from the general din and brawl.

Early in the morning, the jailed were brought out three at a time to be sentenced and sent back out into the oven-like days of the Central Valley, to sweat out the last of their sickness and work like pallid specters, dragging sacks behind them down the rows of cotton until the blessed darkness brought them rest. Esteban watched them go. He watched cell after cell empty itself of its night occupants until he and Isidro were alone again in the basement cellblock.

Mid-morning, the jailer brought in two bowls of mush and two tin cups of black coffee and set them on the concrete outside the cell. Esteban drew one bowl and one cup through the bars and stood up. He sipped the coffee, lukewarm and bitter, while the jailer studied Isidro on the bench.

He don't want none?

Maybe he's too beat up to eat.

Well. I'll leave it. A man who's hurt should eat to keep up his strength.

Say, I think I know you.

Well, I imagine. Anyone been in this jail the past twenty years knows me.

No, I think I sold you some Corn once.

The jailer grinned, slapped a hand on his belly. You might have done.

I can get you some more.

No you can't. Not from where you at.

Once I'm out I'll get you some.

The jailer looked sharkish and knowing. That might be a while.

When do you think we'll see the judge? You heard?

They tell me you two a special case. Cutting a big man and all.

I didn't cut anyone.

You were there, weren't you?

I didn't cut anyone. Get me in front of a judge, I'll explain.

Oh, you're one of those explainers. Well. Be a cold day in hell before you explain your way out of *this* jail.

Esteban and Isidro were in the cell for three days. Each night, a tide of drunks washed in, and each morning they were sentenced and expelled. Twice a day, the jailer came by with food, but he limited himself to winks and grins and would say nothing about when they might have a hearing.

Esteban paced, watched the half-window change from light to dark to light, tried to think through the decisions that were being made by men more powerful than he as a result of a rich man's son losing a finger—decisions that would determine whether he breathed the free air or not.

From time to time, he looked back at Isidro. He had already begun to hate him. Yet when the jailer left, he picked up the food from the cement floor and placed it on the bench beside the hurt man, helped him slowly and painfully eat.

One afternoon the jailer opened the iron door to the cellblock and let in an old Yurok woman, shapeless in a gray dress of coarse woven wool that hung from her shoulders to her bare ankles and feet, graying hair tangled and hanging hag-like about her face. She carried an old string mop and two steel buckets of water mixed with a pungent disinfectant, and if she was surprised to see two prisoners still occupying a cell when she lifted her head and peered with her rheumy eyes, she did not show it. She was old enough to remember the sea of tules, the run of salmon, the mixed herds of tule elk and antelope on the plains, the deer at forest edge and Grizzly wherever it pleased him. She was old enough to remember the duck and goose that in season had blackened the sky, the egret and heron and crane that fished in the marshes, the great sheet of lake that took its color from the sky, grew with the mountains' bounty of water then shrank again. And she was old enough to remember and speak the language that rendered the land and made it knowable. Surely she thought that what she saw when she came to clean the cells for her weekly bread was fantastical, inconceivable. That men would cage other men, then order them to toil on land that had always been hidden by the widespreading water—strange and mad. Surely she thought her language and memory were more real.

But if she thought any of this, her face betrayed nothing. She shuffled down the corridor between the cells, opening one cell after another and sluicing down the cracked cement floors and mopping up the muck and mire, the filth and feculence of a week's worth of jailed men. She spread the sharp smell of disinfectant, sloshing water in, catching it in the strings of her mop and wringing it out by hand, dumping and refilling the buckets at a deep sink near the blank metal door.

When she came to the cell where Esteban and Isidro were held, she proceeded as though they were not there. She unlocked the cell door and tipped her bucket forward, and Esteban stepped onto the hard bench beside Isidro to keep his boots dry. She scuffed into the room, poked her mop into the corners and then twisted the dripping strings with her hands and wrung the filth into her bucket.

Esteban looked through the open cell to the blank door at the end of the cellblock, but he did not think to threaten the old woman or use her as a hostage to escape. He knew the jailer would value her life as less than the escape of a criminal, considering the special case he and Isidro had become. When she finished their cell floor, she closed and locked the barred door behind her, and Esteban leaned against the bars, ran his hand up and down the cold metal and felt the shallow pits against his fingertips.

That night, after the Yurok woman had come and gone, after the cellblock door had been opened to let her out and then locked behind her, no drunks were brought in. The light faded in the basement well window, and the day sounds of the square outside changed to night sounds, slow-moving automobiles and loud talk and the distant music of horns and accordions, but the door was not opened and the ordinary misery of tramps and drunks did not enter the jail. Esteban's tin cup and emptied plate of beans had not been retrieved, and they waited by his feet while the window blackened. He picked up the cup, watched the three bare suspended lightbulbs on the corridor. It was a Thursday, a night no less apt for jailing than Tuesday or Wednesday, and in the courthouse belfry the bell tolled nine, and ten, and eleven, summoning as before the unfortunate to be caged and judged. But none came, and the cells adjoining Esteban and Isidro's remained vacant, bars of shadow striping the bare floors.

When the bell struck midnight and the door remained sealed, the electric lights were cut and the darkness was thick and sudden. Esteban began to rattle the cup back and forth against the dumb bars and shout at the unseen hand that had dropped the lights. He called for the door to open, he shouted that those who had broken the law should be here, not he who had never done harm to anyone, and he shouted that the jail should be full of everyone except for him, that he would see the judge, he would see the judge now, right now.

Behind him as he shouted, Isidro sat silent on the bench. He had remained mute for the three days they had been jailed below ground, his scourged skin weeping, his face darkening with bruises as the swelling lessened. When nobody came at Esteban's rattle and bawl, he turned to Isidro.

I should take this tin cup, he said. Instead of against the bars, I should run it across your teeth. I should smash your head against the wall, finish the job Mr. Glover started.

Isidro raised his head. He was barely visible, a dark tangle of rags against a darker wall.

It's your madness that buried us both, Esteban continued. I should barter your dead body for my freedom. Perhaps that is what they hope for on the other side of the door.

It doesn't matter, Isidro said.

What? He speaks? Esteban gestured broadly to a nonexistent audience. Look! He speaks!

It doesn't matter anymore.

Yes? Esteban crouched close to Isidro, playing as though every word he pronounced were precious. And why does it not matter?

I will never see my son again.

Why? You don't know that.

My Helena. I will never again touch her hand, I know.

Quiet, you. Esteban took his arm and shook it, and Isidro looked up at him with dark eyes. You know none of this.

I know. I know.

How? How do you know?

I have been praying. Three days. And there is no answer.

Better you had prayed that you'd not cut a rich man. Now it is too late.

Too late. You're right. It's too late for me, forever.

Esteban walked back over to the bars, peered at the dim rectangle of window.

Why are they leaving us alone, in the dark? he asked.

In that moment, the lights in the corridor blinked on. Esteban covered his eyes, and the blank metal door began to scrape open.

Even in the basement jail, lit only by naked bulbs, Diamond's face and hair were shining, his pale white-skinned cheeks and cropped blonde hair bright in the dimness. He carried the same ring of keys as the Yurok woman, and they chinked quietly against each other as he padded down the corridor and stopped in front of the cell.

Esteban crouched, tense and waiting. Diamond licked his teeth, and his open mouth was black and awful.

You're in a fix, Esteban. You want out of it?

Not any way you've got.

You think some other way out is coming?

Let me see Judge Harkin. I never cut anyone.

You? You want the judge? You want justice? I don't think

so. If nothing else, you'd be a year in the county work farm for selling intoxicants. But I'm guessing, say what you will, you've cut someone some time or other. You really want justice?

That's not what I'm in for.

How about it, Esteban? How many men you cut? How many men did you take money from? A man like you doesn't want justice.

What do you want me to do?

Easy. I'll open the cell door and you get him on his feet and walk him to the car. Then you drive us somewhere.

Where?

You'll find out.

What are they paying you for this, Diamond?

I won't lie. They're paying me something extra.

What are they paying me?

You? They're paying you your bail. Out of the slammer without seeing Old Thirty-Days-in-the-High-Cotton Harkin. And they're paying you your life back, running drink to the camps.

What if I don't believe you?

Diamond held up the ring of keys, rattled them like teeth, like bones.

Don't go simple on me, Esteban. What choice you got?

From the room outside the cellblock, the bloated jailer's voice came in complaining that his wrists hurt, that his shoulders were killing him.

What choice you got? Diamond did not ask without knowing the answer. Esteban knew that justice in the courtroom would not be for Isidro, nor for him. He knew the weapon Diamond carried under his jacket, an Army Colt that had already killed men in the Philippines and California. And he knew he had to follow Diamond until some way opened up for him that he could not now foresee.

All right.

Esteban hoisted Isidro to his feet and stood by his side, an arm around his back. Diamond drew his pistol, then unlocked the barred door and pushed it open and stood back. Esteban and Isidro made an awkward four-legged creature leading up the corridor, Isidro's feet half-scraping along the rough floor, followed by Diamond carrying his pistol upheld like a candle. They passed through the cellblock door and into the little office where the jailer sat with his arms pinioned behind the back of his swivel chair. The jailer turned left and right and his chair creaked as he witnessed them pass, and he told Diamond that he'd better get someone down to free him before too long, but Diamond paid him no attention.

Esteban and Isidro faced the iron staircase, each step a grate of iron, and step by step Esteban lifted his wounded other half out of the basement jail. The door at the top of the stair was open and the marble-floored hallways of the courthouse were echoing and empty. At a word from Diamond, Esteban slow-walked Isidro through the rotunda, toward the main entrance.

Outside, they walked on the large granite flagstones and under the frieze of blind Justice. Esteban staggered down the broad stairs to street level, Isidro beside him like the burden of his past that grew heavier with each step of time and would grow heavier by night's end. Diamond was behind them, his face shining in the streetlights, his pistol pointing toward heaven with a smooth metallic sheen. There was no traffic on the street in front of the courthouse, no patrol cars, as though by plot or design. At the end of the walkway, a '28 Dodge was parked.

Esteban half-turned his head.

That my car?

You wouldn't want to drive anyone else's, would you?

Esteban last saw his Dodge from the back seat of the patrol car taking him and Isidro to the basement jail, last saw it shining darkly from the floodlights, growing small below the big windowless side of the gin house until it was snuffed from sight. He hadn't expected to see it again, but now that he did, he felt uneasy.

How'd it get here?

You had to give up your key when you went into the cooler, didn't you? Well, it's in the ignition, and your wallet's in the glovebox.

You want to make my car the meat wagon.

I don't see anyone dead. You see anyone dead?

No.

Then shut up and get him into the front seat. I'll sit right behind you.

On the road, Diamond gave brief, one-syllable directions. Left. Left now. Right. Slow down. Right here. They left Lux by streets lined with quiet, secretive houses, shuttered warehouses, an auto lot closed for the day. They avoided roads lit with streetlamps, the town square with the gazebo, the movie theater with the underside of its marquee a small sky of frosted bulbs above the ticket booth. They avoided any avenue where one might spy in and wonder at the trio in the car, the driver's gravedigger face, the face of the passenger clownishly misshapen and discolored, the white man in the back with the barrel of the pistol held solicitously over the top of the front seat.

Outside of town, they funneled onto a two-lane blacktopped road, the only road heading south that was not dirt and gravel. It was called the Bakersfield Road, though no sign designated it as such, simply because in time it would join Highway 99, the spine road of the entire Central Valley, and it was the route that trucks took to and from city markets. The headlights of the car cast an oblong loom of light ahead of them, and all around the fields of cotton were flat and dark and dumb, the darkness of the fields flooding back in behind the car as soon as it passed, and not even the fires of worker camps or the lights of a farmhouse pricked the night.

The road was straight as only human artifice could make it, and Esteban drove seeing a featureless globe of light before him, as though the car were moving not at all. Behind him, Diamond settled back into the seat and moved the barrel of the pistol toward Isidro.

Why did you want to help this guy? he asked.

His son was sick.

That's no reason. What good did your help do his son?

None, I guess.

That's right. None. All you did was help him toward the hell he was headed for anyway. You're going to be glad to be through with him, aren't you?

I don't know. I don't know if I will be through with him.

You will be. Tonight. And you can go back to selling *vino*, and forget about ever having tried to help anyone.

That's good. That's all I want.

There's the old Esteban.

Diamond reached into his shirt pocket and pulled out an open pack of cigarettes, shook one halfway out and took it between his lips. He lowered the pistol briefly to strike a match, then raised it again.

Hey. He ever talk?

Not much.

Diamond began to prod at Isidro with the barrel of the gun like he was a caged circus bear, a formerly fearsome beast who could still be roused to give some entertainment.

Hey you. What's going on in there?

Esteban felt the wounded man stir beside him. He wondered if Isidro was seeing visions of his son.

Hey. You ever think about where you were going when you set foot in that gin building?

Isidro moved his head from side to side, slow and heavy, though whether he was responding to the question or to some passion quickening inside him was impossible to say.

You ever think about it? Well I'll tell you. You were headed right for here. Once your foot was on that path, there was only one place it led to. This car. This night. You going where you're going.

Diamond prodded again, and Isidro breathed deeply within his chest, something between a growl and a sigh.

And hoping there was help to be had from Esteban? I could have told you better than that. Esteban aims mostly to help himself. Right, Esteban?

That's right. Esteban spoke without expression.

You almost brought him along. But he's too smart for that. So you're going where we're all going. And you're going like we all go. Alone.

Isidro spoke. I know, he said.

You know?

I know. There is no hope to be had. Not in Esteban, not in anyone.

Diamond laughed. Maybe you know Esteban better than I thought.

A false calm settled inside the car. Esteban straightened

up as the hum of the tires and engine became again the only sound in the quiet.

Slow now, Diamond said.

They approached a side road where two parked cars waited, and Diamond told Esteban to pull over. Esteban downshifted, and before he came to a complete stop, the doors of the cars winged open and men were standing and blinking in the headlights, dressed in suits and vests, large and washed colorless in the harsh glare.

Cut the lights, Diamond said. Engine too. Cut 'em.

Esteban turned off the lights and killed the engine, but he had already seen something that he wished he had not, and the instant of seeing and recognizing was not to be wished away or undone.

In the headlights, he had seen Mr. Joshua Glover, Aaron's father, the owner of the drained lakebed where Camp Olvido lay, the owner of thousands of acres of cotton north and south and east of Lux. Esteban had seen him before, in the Cotton Festival on Main Street, on the back of a deep-chested horse, looking down at those who came to the parade with the horseman's natural air of superiority. Now Esteban had seen him in the light, standing in suit and hat, stiff gray moustache on his lip, broad hands like spades held before him as though to gather in his due.

Esteban had seen him, standing first among the others, and he knew that Diamond had seen him by the same light, and he knew that Diamond knew that he had seen.

You stay put, Diamond said.

Esteban sat and did not speak while Diamond stepped out of the Dodge, pulled the moribund Isidro upright out of the passenger's seat, and kicked both doors shut behind him. Before the windshield, the eyes of flashlights blinked on, multiple eyes like a pack of wolves, mobbing together then separating, always in motion. Once, Esteban saw the lights join and pin themselves to Isidro, his face pale and already spectral in the concentrated light, held for display and made visible as a thief's would be before a public lashing. Then the lights separated again before joining together, lancing through the windshield and eyeing Esteban's face from three angles. Esteban felt himself studied from beyond those lights by an intelligence that belonged to no individual man wielding the light but rather an intelligence shared and native to those who are stronger when grasping those who are weaker. He kept his head bowed, did not attempt to see past the battery of lights to the faces of those who held them, which would in any case have been impossible. His gaze was lowered, submissive to their inspection, and remained so even after the lights removed themselves from scrutinizing him and resumed their restless buzzing.

Then the lights drew together, grew compact in a line and moved, as if by a single urge, toward the cars. The wands of light all angled downwards, turned the gravel alongside the road the color of old bones.

A few yards out, the flashlights were all snuffed, and the black was regnant, and there was no light at all. Esteban raised his head but he could see nothing, and what he could hear was only an absence of sound, formless and impossible to interpret. He felt the steering wheel within his hands, felt the grain of polished wood beneath his fingertips. He raised his hands to his face and felt the deep lines beside his mouth, his *chato* nose, his moustache, as though feeling the boundary between his body and the outside dark.

The first alteration was the noise of car doors opened and clipped shut again. The engines cranked on, loud suddenly and dinning, and then headlight beams crossed the roadway, and in the smear of light, on the blacktop, Esteban could see the body of Isidro.

He waited for the cars to leave, to pull out onto the road and fly back to that other world where they lived, and leave him to this world. He waited for them to pull out so that he could know that they would not come for him. But they did not move. Two cars, their outlines visible now in the ambient light of their own headlights, crouched and still.

A single flashlight pinned through the passenger side window and lit up Esteban's face, then the door opened.

You're still here. Good man.

Diamond slid into the passenger's seat, and there was no sign of the gun. Esteban sat still in the driver's seat.

Now, Diamond said. Start the car.

We heading back to Lux?

When I say. Put the car in gear and ease it straight forward.

Esteban closed his eyes, lowered his head so that he would not see. He let out the clutch, and the Dodge moved slowly forward.

The right front tire bumped up and over the body. Then the right rear tire bumped over.

Brake it, Diamond said.

Esteban stopped the car and looked at Diamond, and

looked past him to the two sets of headlights lidless and glaring.

Now. Put it in reverse. Slow and easy does it.

Again, in reverse, the right tires of the Dodge rode up and down, one by one, shuddering the car.

Brake, Diamond said.

Esteban pushed in the clutch and hit the brake and waited. From one of the cars, a single horn sounded, quick and sharp, not like a horn at all but like a shriek.

Okay. That should do it. Turn the car around and let's head back.

Esteban cranked the wheel, heard the rubber crawl on the blacktop, then pulled the Dodge north, toward Lux. Behind him, from the two black cars, nobody descended to inspect at close range the roadway. First one car then the other re-gained the road and sped south, toward Bakersfield, the Grapevine, Los Angeles, hurtling away from the scene fash-ioned by their vengeance.

Esteban drove without speaking north on Bakersfield Road, drove without looking at Diamond in the seat beside him, as though, if silent, he could play the dumb and blind instrument of what had occurred, a simple tool in the hands of others with no will or complicity. A look to the right, where Diamond sat, would be a look to where Isidro had been on the journey out and force a recognition of Isidro's absence that Esteban was unwilling to face. If he looked, Diamond would look back at him and would say without speaking: You were apt for the task. You knew what was required of you, and you did it.

He heard the Colt, the almost silent sound of metal slipping from leather, and he knew that Diamond had the pistol out, was checking it with his eyes and hands, then seating it again in his holster. The pistol did not smell of burned gunpowder, a smell Esteban knew, and he knew that they had not needed a bullet when his car would serve.

He did not speak until they broke through the city limits of Lux, and then he asked where to.

Drop me off in front of the courthouse. Same place we started from.

Same place I escaped from?

You didn't escape. You were just let go. No charges against you. Because you didn't do anything wrong. Did you, Esteban?

No. I guess I didn't.

Well then. Case closed.

So. Who were those men out there?

Diamond gave a quick snort, both at the impossibility of Esteban not having known and recognized the shape of Mr. Joshua Glover rising into the glare of the headlights and at the audacity of Esteban thinking he could fool him with such an obvious ruse. Mr. Glover had been overeager, no doubt, stupid to show himself large and obvious in the light with the brass buttons on his vest and the brush moustache and heavy-fleshed face. But in Diamond's reckoning, this was not a problem for Mr. Glover, but for Esteban.

You don't need to worry about that, he said. Not yet, anyway.

Maybe better I don't know.

Yeah. Maybe. Diamond spoke in a tone that let Esteban know that they both knew he was talking bullshit.

Esteban pulled the Dodge onto Court Street and parked in front of the broad granite walkway that led to the staircase and the pillared entryway of the courthouse. He set the brake, left the engine running.

Diamond got out, then leaned back into the open door.

You get some sleep. You need to be back to work tomorrow. Your customers are thirsty.

He slammed the door shut. Esteban drove to the end of the block and turned left, to East Lux. Until he crossed the railroad tracks, he expected to be stopped, caught in the act of escaping from jail. He could be sent away to prison, he could die in a gun battle, he could be removed and the matter closed completely. But nothing happened, and as he bumped over the railroad tracks he thought of that other un-speakable object he'd bumped over and thought that per-haps he was a witness who could be left alive, since he was a witness who would never be believed, a witness who, in his car and with his hands on the wheel and a foot on the gas pedal, had crushed the remainder of life from Isidro.

- -

Early the next morning, a solitary truck rolled south on the Bakersfield Road. A low and chilling fog lay over the land, and the sun was rising but the light it gave was faint and bloodlike and wavery, and it gave no heat at all. The truck, one of many that would go down the road that day, was loaded with burlap sacks of yellow onions, to be sold in the Bakersfield market.

As the truck traveled, a flock of dark birds rose suddenly through the red-tinged mist, and for a moment the wind-shield and windows were veiled by black and milling wings and sharp beaks. Then the truck hit a mound, jumped air-borne for a moment amid the murderous flock, and jarred itself back to the ground.

The truck braked and stopped. Behind it, the swirl of birds had settled again on the pavement, dark wings and heads faint and muted in the low fog.

A man in overalls got down from the truck, walked to his four tires and looked in the wheel wells and inspected the springs. Then he walked back to the gathering of birds. They croaked and scolded him, unwilling to give up their find, but he walked through them and battered the air with his arms and they rose into the mist and settled again not far distant.

The man crouched and looked at the body. It lay in the attitude of a penitent, with hands folded together at the end of outstretched arms, head bowed down, prostrate on the road and facing the thin red sun. He saw that the body did not breathe, and he stood and pushed it with his boot. The body had stiffened the way all flesh does, and the stiffness, along with the birds, told him that his truck had not killed this man.

He picked up the body like a bale of hay and loaded it onto the flatbed of his truck and with a hank of rope lashed it alongside his sacks of onions. Then, although it would make him an hour late to the wholesale vegetable market, he turned the truck around and headed back toward Lux.

- -

Isidro's family sent every day to the jail to see if he was sentenced to work in the fields, sentenced to the same life he'd had before. One man in town who spoke English, a connection from their home village in Michoacán, went to ask if Isidro Rulfo had yet seen the judge, and when he could be seen, and was every day turned away.

On the fourth day, the man went to the black door at the back of the courthouse, the door that led down to the basement jail. He knocked timidly, and the door lurched open, and the jailer on duty, large and owlish with round glasses and a red-and-gray scruff around his bald head, cocked his head at the inquiry as though he needed to hear the question more clearly.

Who's that?

Isidro Rulfo.

No. No Isidro Rulfo in my jail.

Has he seen the judge? Do you know where he is?

Can't tell you nothing about him. Far as I know, no Isidro Rulfo has ever been in this jail.

But Señor . . . yesterday, he was here.

The jailer on duty cocked his large head, frowned in a puzzled way.

You telling me I don't know who is or who is not in my own jail?

No, Señor . . .

Good. Well. I expect your man is lying around town somewhere. Drunk, like as not. You best look for him elsewhere.

The man nodded and went to the morgue below the police station and there found a body beneath a sheet with its arms stiff and outstretched and uncovered, extending out beyond the cheap shroud. The body's face was scourged from the pavement, but his clothing, stained dark with oil and rubber and blood and urine, accorded with what the man knew of Isidro. He had understood the jailer to tell him to look here, and he had found what he was looking for.

Isidro was buried in a pauper's graveyard in East Lux, an unkempt section of the main cemetery unshaded by any trees and bare of the stones and monuments inscribed with the deeds of the founding generation. A Portuguese priest from Five Wounds came for charity's sake and said words over the pine box as Helena, dressed in the black she'd been prepared for, sat in the single wooden chair with her still-living child. Behind her stood Isidro's father and the small clutch of mourners who could leave work for an afternoon and see buried one who would never come closer to home than now he was.

- -

Esteban began again making his rounds. He drove to the distillery hidden in the Isabella Valley and loaded up with brandy and casks of wine and sold to the bars and pool halls of East Lux, then went again to the distillery and drove to the labor camps and set up his poor makeshift bar in the early evening as pickers returned from long days with the sack around their necks. Everyone he met knew he had been in jail, knew that Isidro died while he yet lived, and no one spoke of it. They treated him as though he were both fearsome and polluted, as though he were now in the protection of the big men and offending him would bring disaster upon them, and as though he had the mark upon him and befriending him would afflict them with the same curse. They bought from him, as before, but they bought with caution and suspicion.

Esteban had seen this look before. When he was thirteen, he'd come north from Jalisco with his father and mother and two sisters to escape the wars and soon learned that the work available to a Mexican required a bent back and low-ered head. Then, laying railroad tracks in Arizona, he caught the eye of a vendor who followed the workers with two mules and a cart. A man who always laughed, who always wore striped shirts and red suspenders to hold up the pants around his well-fed belly, who sold dried chiles and choco-lates and other items not sold in the company store, along with opiates in small vials as medicine to take away the pains of working *el traque*. Esteban left his family to go with the vendor, work as his *mozo de mulas*, and never return to stoop labor.

When the vendor turned from the road gang and headed back to Nogales for supplies, Esteban went with him. In the evening, around the campfire, the vendor encouraged Este-ban to drink doped wine with him, laughing as he always laughed, telling him that it would make a man of him. The wine made Esteban sleepy, and he rolled into his blanket near the fire while the vendor laughed at him for being young. Later, when the fire was burned down to its embers, Esteban groggily sensed the vendor crouching above him, huge and naked and hairless, his striped shirt unbuttoned and his red suspenders slipped off his shoulders so that his pants were around his knees. He stripped the blanket from Esteban, embraced him in his large fleshiness, seemed to cover him completely in his fire-warmed flesh. The embrace lasted a drugged and indeterminate time. Then Esteban heard the snap of suspenders moving back in place, and the vendor rolled Esteban back into the blankets before heaving himself up to sleep in the wagon.

Esteban rode with the vendor for one year, with the same thing happening whenever the wagon was out from the work camps and still distant from the city. In that year, Esteban learned about all the vendor's stores, where he bought and from whom in the city, who was bribed among the whites at the work camps to be allowed to sell his goods, the powders and liquors he mixed to sell in small vials of colored glass. Esteban set himself to learn English, and to learn to read and write, which the vendor was happy to help with. As they traveled, sitting together on the bench seat of the wagon, Esteban holding the reins, the vendor would hold forth in English about his life and business, and he bought a copy of

Oliver Twist for Esteban to study through, thinking no doubt that he was purchasing the boy's happiness and loyalty without realizing that he was making him the master of all his store of knowledge.

Near the middle of summer, when Esteban was fourteen and stronger and nearly as tall as the vendor, they camped in the high desert under a clear sky. The unseeing eyes of stars swam over them, and the whited band of the Milky Way, diffuse light of stars too distant to distinguish, spanned from blank horizon to blank horizon, and the earth was smooth and lifted up, like an altartop in the middle of which a tiny fire burned, the campfire near the wagon. Esteban had mixed powder into a bottle of wine, and he pretended to drink it himself, holding his tongue against the mouth of the bottle, before passing it over. The vendor drank and laughed, and his cheeks were fat and flushed and painted red by the firelight, and he slapped his hand against his good round belly to show that he was happy. Esteban opened another bottle of wine, and they began a kind of drinking game, encouraging each other to drink under the empty watchfulness of the sky until the vendor finally slept, overcome by his drugged potion.

Esteban stood over him, swayed slightly. The vendor lay

face up, mouth open so that his chin pushed into his fleshy throat. The stripes of his shirt and his red suspenders were black in the light, and he breathed loudly from his dark mouth, blowing his stubbled ruddy cheeks in and out.

From the wagon, Esteban plucked the large sheath knife that he first had seen when he began to travel with the vendor, the knife the vendor wore on his belt when money was changing hands at remote railroad camps. Esteban grasped the knife by the handle, as though it were a staff, and walked unsteadily back to where the vendor lay. The vendor's eyes were still closed and his mouth still open, and he snorted and coughed as he breathed his drugged sleep.

Esteban knelt beside the large-bodied man, padded by fat, filling out his clothes, lying sleek and corpulent. Where would the heart lie within such a body?

He raised the vendor's knife and plunged it straight down into the vendor's throat, through the windpipe and one artery, until he felt it nick one of the neckbones deep within.

The vendor bolted up with his eyes amazed, breathing in his own blood. He clawed upward, grasping at something he couldn't see, and stood on his feet. He tried to call Esteban's name for help but was choking on his own blood, and he staggered in a circle around the fire with the hilt of the knife sticking from his throat like a grotesque other tongue. Esteban stayed several steps away, backing from him in a rough circle, watching and waiting. When the vendor found the knife, he pulled it from himself with a lurid sucking sound and looked at it stupidly as blood jetted from his throat. He recognized it, and took a step toward the boy he thought he had known.

Esteban backed away. The vendor dropped the knife and put both hands to his throat, trying to gather up his lost blood and bind up the rent flesh, trying to find a way to keep breathing the earth's sweet air.

He fell to his knees, then his muscles sagged and he toppled over, and the great bag of skin that had contained him slackened and emptied. Esteban knelt again beside him and watched his eyes as they filmed over and seemed to flatten slightly as he entered definitively into the land of the dead. And Esteban sat back and wept, because the vendor had felt a kind of love for him, and now he was beloved by no one.

In the morning, he used a mule to drag the vendor's body to the edge of a dry arroyo and tumbled it over the edge, and it rolled a dozen feet down until caught by the rough eroded sandstone and the mesquite and trident sage. Then he hitched up the wagon and followed the same route as the vendor had, catching up to the track gangs slowly extending the railroad across the desert. The white company men he bribed didn't care that he was not the same one who had bribed them the month before. The money was still green. But the trackworkers who were his customers, men like the father he never saw again, looked at him cautiously. Perhaps they recognized the knife he wore on his belt and knew him to be a killer of men. Still, they bought what they needed, and Esteban learned to laugh and joke with them while staying distant and watchful. He kept trade with the track crews until they reached San Bernardino, then sold the mules and wagon and bought a car and began selling liquor.

The look he now saw in the labor camps from cotton pickers was the same he had seen then. They came to the back of his Dodge, they bought wine and brandy, they built a fire to sit at while they drank. But they did not ask what had happened, how two men had been in a jail cell and one had ended with dirt covering his eyes forever and the other free and untouched. Some few, at least, saw him and determined to drink no more, to save their money this year and find work in Los Angeles and a place to stay, to leave off wandering the landscape in search of a harvest that would always belong to another. They saw his dead flat eyes, saw him feeding off them like the dead harvester of souls, saw Isidro as his prey and chose to be his prey no longer. But others, more, wanted what he sold, wanted the ring of drink and talk that came with him.

- -

Two weeks after Isidro was buried, Esteban drove down the rutted lane again to Camp Olvido, and as he drove he sounded his two-toned horn, the horn that announced it was Esteban coming and nobody else. He sounded the horn pridefully, like a person with no fear or shame, and he rounded his Dodge into the small clearing near the oxen shed. Some children ran away as he got out of the car, ducked back into the warren of mud-colored tents and cardboard huts, but he ignored them and opened up the trunk and set up his barrel of Jackass brandy. The sky overhead was a dull, dusky purple, big and empty, and to the west a smudge of rose ran the low horizon. Amid the tents and huts, little cooking fires sent up sparks and trickles of smoke.

Esteban waited, his arms folded, leaning back against the car fender. He wore a knife at his belt, though not the one he'd had before, not the one that had cropped off Aaron

Glover's finger, the very one that had killed the vendor. He pulled the new knife out after a time and dug at the dirt below his fingernails and watched the sky darken.

Then a gang of men walked forth from among the tents, half a dozen all dressed in jeans and workshirts and boots. They walked together, like a deputation, and Esteban straightened up, alert and poised. At their head, Helena's brother walked, and they stopped near Esteban and formed a small drift of men, half-surrounding him.

Buenas noches. Esteban put the knife away slowly, as though without concern.

Muy buenas, Helena's brother said.

Esteban looked from face to face, all men he had sold drink to in the past, all now closed-mouthed and somber. He did not see the old man among them, Isidro's father.

How is Helena?

How could she be? She is grieving.

And the child? Manuel?

Helena's brother opened his hands. He lives. It is as though his father's spirit has come down to give him strength.

He's well?

Not well. But he lives.

I'm glad. May he grow up and be strong.

We wanted to—Helena's brother broke off speech and could not find the resolve to finish the sentence he'd begun. Esteban looked at the others.

Yes?

We wanted to thank you.

It was one of the others who spoke. Helena's brother was looking down, and he put a fist to his mouth.

Thank me for what?

For what you tried to do for Isidro.

What?

Helena's brother spoke again. You led him to a big man to plead for his son. It wasn't you who pulled the knife. And in jail, you tried to keep him alive, make sure he ate. We heard this. If you had been able to keep him from being killed, you would have, I know. Now his spirit blesses you.

The other men slowly nodded, their faces solemn under their white straw hats, and they murmured soft sounds of agreement and approval.

Helena also wishes to see you, to thank you. We were waiting. We said, We are waiting for him and we know he will come. We are waiting, and Manuel is waiting until Esteban comes, so that Esteban can see him and pass on his father's blessing.

Esteban turned from them and filled cups from the barrel of brandy and handed them around, and he took one himself, something he never did while selling at the camps. They all drank, and Esteban filled everyone's glass again.

I don't deserve your thanks, he said. I would have done better for him if I'd not taken him anywhere, not even given him money that wouldn't get him a real doctor, just left him out here to hope and pray.

That's just what the old man said you would say, one of the gang said. Isidro's father. He said you'd deny ever doing any good.

Well, he's right. Did he say you should believe me when I denied it?

He didn't say one way or the other.

He should have.

Come. The old man is waiting with Helena to see you. As soon as he heard the horn, he went to her side to wait for you.

What if I don't want to see him? Esteban asked. But he joined the group of men walking down into camp, and he took the cask of brandy with him. As they walked, more men noticed the cask Esteban carried, noticed that he poured for all without asking for pay. He was stopped twice on the way by men crowding around and asked to pour, which he did willingly for all who had a cup, and drank again himself, so that by the time he approached Helena he came at the head of a small parade of merriment, as though he were leading a celebratory march after some obscure victory. Helena stood by a small fire before one of the warped cardboard shacks, full-skirted in black with a black widow's crown covering her hair. Manuel, the child, was leaning against her, looking out then folding himself back into the rough cloth of her skirt and hiding his face against her.

Esteban stumbled to a stop before her, and the men following him bunched into a jumble then filtered out to each side, so that Esteban stood at the head of a drunken band, standing with the keg held against his body like a mockery of an offering. Helena stroked the brown hair of her son, then slowly turned his head with her fingers so that he was looking out at the men around them, at Esteban standing splay-footed and open-mouthed.

Look, she said, there is the man who comes to you from your father, who comes to give you his blessing.

Esteban gaped at the little boy, who looked at him thin and wizened, his eyes still too large for his shrunken face, too old for his years. The boy leaned back into his mother's skirts, silent and waiting.

The old man, Isidro's father, came to Helena's side, his mouth a straight unsmiling line.

Did he say anything before he died?

Say anything?

You were there. You must know.

Esteban looked about him at the faces of the men who surrounded him, as though one of them out of good fellowship would supply what was required.

Whatever he said last to you, Helena said. It would be a message to Manuel. And myself.

There is no hope to be had . . . Esteban felt a hand pat him on his shoulder, the brother's hand, to comfort him and strengthen him as he recalled a time of great pain. Everyone waited; even those who had followed down for drink now wanted the words that would make their drink a ceremony of remembrance.

I cannot recall exactly what he said. But he talked about hoping his son would grow up tall and strong.

The crowd sighed, a sound content and fulfilled. Helena looked at him from within the dark frame of her widow's headscarf.

Nothing else? Nothing to me? Did he say my name?

Not in anyone . . .

No. Esteban shook his head. That's all. I'm sorry.

Well. It is enough.

She bowed her head down to Manuel, who was still studying Esteban with his overlarge eyes.

You see? Your father was thinking of you at the last, hoping for you to grow well.

The old man looked at Esteban, bitter and doubting. And how did he die, finally? Can you tell us?

It was nighttime. I can't be certain. That is the truth.

The old man's eyes lit with knowledge, perhaps understanding that if Esteban had to claim a statement as true, it showed that everything else had a shadow of falsehood. He was about to speak again when Esteban, to forestall more questions, held up the keg of brandy.

Let's drink, he said. When we lose one like Isidro, those who remain can help each other, gather together, raise the children. Let's drink. And we'll drink to hope, to seeing Manuel grown tall and strong.

The men around him, who had followed him and his open keg, crowded about with shouts and cries, and he poured for all. When the keg was empty, he sent boys for all the bottles of wine he had in the Dodge, and they returned, six boys with smooth green bottles clutched by both arms against their thin chests. He gave each boy a nickel, and began to open the bottles and pass them around.

Before them, at the center of the rude celebration, Helena stood with Manuel, the child with his face again in her skirts, looking out from time to time as the men grew louder. Then, at a word from the old man, Helena withdrew with the child, and the men continued to drink and shout around a space now empty of the object of their celebration, the young widow and the child of the next generation to be raised up. Someone brought some firewood to the small cooking fire that Helena had been tending, and the fire grew bright and tall, and the night became like other nights when Esteban came by Camp Olvido and brought drink, but better, because the drink was free.

Esteban opened bottle after bottle, drank straight from the bottle until the harsh red wine washed his throat and spilled from the corners of his mouth, then handed it around. The first bottles went fast, but as the drinking slowed he opened more and swore that as long as there were men to drink, he would not leave a single bottle unopened.

A guitar was found, and some young women came out and began to dance with men around the fire. They danced and sang, songs from Jalisco and Michoacán and Sonora, *corridos* celebrating Gregorio Cortés or older songs in praise of Joaquín. Esteban sang along, and drank, and would have been able to forget how the evening had begun if not for the old man, who remained after Helena and Manuel had gone. He remained but stood apart, thin and bitter, like an accusing angel, and when the bottles were passed his way he refused them all, because he would not drink to a lie.

- -

The fires were long out, and the wine drunk, and Camp Olvido lay quiet and stuporous, dazed by the sudden sense of surfeit and pleasure, a sense that was already passing away in the uneasy drunken sleep of men and women under canvas or low cardboard roofs. In the Dodge, Esteban had stretched out in the back seat and dozed, conscious of the cold but ignoring it. He had his canvas jacket on backwards so that it tented shallowly over his body like a makeshift blanket, and when he felt a chill he shifted and crossed his arms more tightly across his chest.

An hour before sunrise, he heard through his shallow dream the car door creak open. He ignored it. Then he felt each leg lifted, and he was pulled straight out from the car seat, and his head clipped the running board and thudded to the ground, and he lay supine, gazing up at the risen winter stars and gulping for air like a boated fish.

A boot pushed him in the ribs, and he felt a hand scramble into his pockets.

Where are the keys? a voice asked.

He rolled to all fours, away from the probing hand, but the boot shoved him again to the ground.

Who? he asked. Who is it? He looked up but could see only two featureless men against the black sky.

It's us. Policarpo and Nivardo.

The Del Río brothers laughed. They had played sneak-cups during the evening, and were sober and awake. When Esteban tried to rise again, Nivardo pushed him down.

What do you want?

Your key.

What, are you thieves? You're going to steal my car?

No, Policarpo said. We're going to buy.

Buy my car?

No. Buy your business.

My business? Esteban rolled upright and got to his knees, and this time the brothers let him. He wheezed in the cold black, bent over with his hands on his thighs and heaved up a burning string of alcohol. Then he wiped his mouth on his sleeve, thinking he needed to think clearly because a mistake now would not be undone.

My business, he said, is not for sale.

We did not buy it from you. We bought it from Diamond.

We bought it from Diamond, Nivardo echoed.

Esteban knew without feeling that the knife at his belt was gone, and he saw in the shades before him that each was carrying a knife.

There's no need to buy from Diamond. I was already thinking, after last night, that I need some help. In Isabella Valley, I have waiting twelve cases and six kegs that I've already paid for. You can help me deliver it, and we'll split the money we make.

One of the men, Nivardo, looked at his brother, who shook his head.

And there's money I'm owed at bars and camps all around Lux. They won't pay you without me there.

Whiskey debts, Policarpo said. They are never paid. We will start from nothing.

No. You will start from less than nothing because you will owe Diamond. What did you pay for my business?

Nivardo laughed. A low price.

A low price?

Your life only.

Esteban felt the weird upon him, as though all his past transgressions were clothing themselves in bones and flesh.

You don't want to kill me, he said. Or I will ride around on your shoulder for all the days of your life, and grow heavier day by day, and one day crush you. Look. The key is hidden inside the cab. I alone can find it in the dark. Drive me to Bakersfield and leave me there, and I will disappear, and you can tell Diamond whatever you want.

Policarpo and Nivardo exchanged looks, each trying to understand what the other was thinking.

Isn't that better than having blood on your hands? Esteban asked.

I wish Diamond had given us a gun, Nivardo said. Then it would be easy.

There's nothing easy.

As they spoke, a strange host rose up behind the two, white-robed and ghostly in the dark, many-headed and walking on silent feet. Esteban saw it and continued to talk to the brothers, claimed that they could trust him never to return since he would have nothing to return for. The host drew closer and raised in the air their whitish cloths while the brothers listened and tried to adjust their plans to the notions pouring forth from Esteban.

At a hiss, the host rushed forward, and the long white robes revealed as cotton sacks were thrown around the two brothers and enveloped them. The two fell together, pushed and pummeled, and they lost their knives and were on the ground beneath the pressing of knees and feet and hands. The old man, standing to one side, cackled with pleasure and directed the men not to strike them if they stopped struggling.

Esteban staggered to his feet, hand on the fender of his car, and looked down at the two brothers. They lay out on their backs, the sacks stretched over their bodies like cerements, though their eyes were wide and live and frightened. An arc of men kneeled about their heads, and other men stood behind, waiting now for a sign.

The old man was at Esteban's side, cautious and watchful. Esteban bent down and picked up his knife and wiped its blade on his jeans. When he did not immediately sheathe it, the old man put a hand on his arm.

This revenge is not for you.

There is no revenge needed.

He squatted close to Policarpo and Nivardo, and he spoke just loud enough for all to hear.

These men have done you a favor, the greatest favor of
your lives. If they had not stopped you, in five years, you,
Policarpo, would have killed your brother. Or the other way
round. And you would have lived with that mark on you forever.

Esteban stood up and slipped his knife into its sheath. To
the east, above the foothills and the distant Sierras, a faint
line of red inscribed itself, a tracing of dawn.

It seems that someone wanted you dead, the old man
said.

And still does. These two were just instruments.

Are you leaving?

Ahorita. And never coming back.

Look. The old man signaled with his finger, and in the
midst of the men stood Helena, with the child Manuel, and
by their feet were two small sacks of their clothing.

Take her, he said. Take her and her child to Milagro Park.
In recompense for what we have done for you. And after, you
can go where you will.

I can't take anyone. I can't help anyone. I'm better alone.

If you don't, you will take shame with you instead. And
guilt. No one is alone.

And Diamond will be following me. Diamond, or someone who is Diamond with another face. It isn't safe.

Is it safe here, in Camp Olvido? Take them with you, to a safe refuge, so that Isidro's hope for his son can come true.

Isidro's hope. It was just an invention of Esteban's that they had believed, that even the old man had believed. But then Manuel, the little boy, left his mother's black skirts and walked between the men, past the two brothers bound up and helpless, and to Esteban's side. His mother, Helena, kneeled down and watched him go. Manuel leaned against Esteban's rough jeans and turned his face up toward him.

My Papa . . .

Yes? Esteban reached down and touched the curled hair on top of the boy's head. The hair was too thin for a boy his age, and the skull was present and mortal beneath Esteban's fingers.

My Papa . . .

He's gone.

Where?

Esteban shook his head, waved Helena forward.

In minutes, Helena's small sacks were in the trunk with the empty cooperage, and she was seated in the front with Manuel held in her lap. Esteban turned the key and the Dodge fired its cylinders and he turned on the headlights. As he swung the car in a wide circle, the lights sliced over Camp

Olvido, illuminated the huddled cardboard roofs and mud-colored canvas tents and tripods of sticks holding up cold cooking pots over extinguished fires. Those who remained watching, the brother and the old man among them, raised their hands in farewell as the Dodge straightened up on the dirt road between the fields.

Esteban looked over at Manuel, whose head was nestled against his mother's breast.

He sleeps already?

Yes. He sleeps.

Good.

They drove the dirt roads, gradually rose out of the drained lakebed, where men had turned rivers and built levees and brought to light the rich hidden land and on it raised stands of cotton. They rose, three of them, in the car that had killed the woman's husband and the boy's father, out of the place that had not forgotten the sea of tules and the silver sheet of water and the patient fishing birds. They rose, and the road breasted the levees, and then they were on the Bakersfield Road, heading south into the long valley.

ACKNOWLEDGMENTS

Some years ago, I worked as a volunteer teaching English to recent immigrants in Watsonville, California. I also spent time along the U.S.-Mexican border, interviewing Border Patrol agents, a coyote, and those seeking to cross into the United States. I know I would not have been able to write this novella without the stories I heard while teaching and freelancing, and I first want to acknowledge all those who spoke to me during those times with such candor and generosity.

My thanks go to the gifted photographer Victor Varela, with whom I shared many travels.

I would like to acknowledge the support of the Institute for the Study of Culture and Society at Bowling Green State University. I would also like to thank my colleagues in the Creative Writing Program and the Department of English at BGSU, especially Wendell Mayo, *el maestro*.

My great thanks and appreciation to Keith Tuma and all the staff at Miami University Press. Jody Bates and Samantha Edmonds were tireless in reading and rereading the manuscript and helping me make some most-needed revisions. And it has been wonderful to work with Amy Toland to bring this book into being. The press is helping to sustain the novella, a literary form that includes some of the world's great works of fiction, and we should all be thankful for that.

Finally, my thanks to Kimberly, for putting up with the sound of a manual typewriter, and for many other things.

ABOUT THE AUTHOR

Lawrence Coates is the author of four novels, most recently *The Goodbye House*. He has received such honors as the Western States Book Award in Fiction and an NEA Fellowship in Fiction. He teaches Creative Writing at Bowling Green State University.